Pumpkins

A Level One Reader

By Cynthia Klingel and Robert B. Noyed

The Child's World®

It is big. It is orange.
It is a pumpkin.

3

This big pumpkin
began as a little seed.

4

The seed is planted in
the ground.

A green plant grows
from the seed.

The sun and rain help the pumpkin plant grow.

The plant is a vine. It spreads over the ground.

Yellow flowers bloom
on the vine.

Each flower becomes
a small pumpkin.
These tiny pumpkins
are still yellow.

18

The pumpkins grow bigger. The pumpkins turn orange.

19

This pumpkin is ready for Halloween or Thanksgiving pie.

Word List

bloom

ground

Halloween

seed

spreads

Thanksgiving

vine

Note to Parents and Educators

Welcome to The Wonders of Reading™! These books provide text at three different levels for beginning readers to practice and strengthen their reading skills. Additionally, the use of nonfiction text provides readers the valuable opportunity to *read to learn*, not just to learn to read.

These leveled readers allow children to choose books at their level of reading confidence and performance. Level One books offer beginning readers simple language, word choice, and sentence structure as well as a word list. Level Two books feature slightly more difficult vocabulary, longer sentences, and longer total text. In the back of each Level Two book are an index and a list of books and Web sites for finding out more information. Level Three books continue to extend word choice and length of text. In the back of each Level Three book are a glossary, an index, and a list of books and Web sites for further research.

State and national standards in reading and language arts emphasize using nonfiction at all levels of reading development. The Wonders of Reading™ fill the historical void in nonfiction material for the primary grade readers with the additional benefit of a leveled text.

About the Authors

Cindy Klingel has worked as a high school English teacher and an elementary teacher. She is currently the curriculum director for a Minnesota school district. Writing children's books is another way for her to continue her passion for sharing the written word with children. Cindy Klingel is a frequent visitor to the children's section of bookstores and enjoys spending time with her many friends, family, and two daughters.

Bob Noyed started his career as a newspaper reporter. Since then, he has worked in communications and public relations for more than fourteen years for a Minnesota school district. He enjoys writing books for children and finds that it brings a different feeling of challenge and accomplishment from other writing projects. He is an avid reader who also enjoys music, theater, traveling, and spending time with his wife, son, and daughter.

Published by The Child's World®, Inc.

PO Box 326
Chanhassen, MN 55317-0326
800-599-READ
www.childsworld.com

Photo Credits
© 1993 Dan Dempster/Dembinsky Photo Assoc. Inc.: 21
© D. Young-Wolff/Photo Edit: 6
© Joel Dexter/Unicorn Stock Photos: 14
© John L. Ebeling/Unicorn Stock Photos: 13
© Kindra Clineff/Tony Stone Images: 18
© 1992 Larime Photographic/Dembinsky Photo Assoc. Inc.: 10
© Leslie Borden/PhotoEdit: 9
© Mitch Kezar/Tony Stone Images: cover
© Myrleen Ferguson/PhotoEdit: 2
© Tom Edwards/ Unicorn Stock Photos: 17
© Tony Stone Worldwide: 5

Project Coordination: Editorial Directions, Inc.
Photo Research: Alice K. Flanagan

Library of Congress Cataloging-in-Publication Data
Klingel, Cynthia Fitterer.
Pumpkins / by Cynthia Klingel and Robert B. Noyed.
p. cm. — (Wonder books)
Summary: Simple text describes pumpkins and how they are grown.
ISBN 1-56766-796-1 (lib. reinforced)
1. Pumpkin—Juvenile literature.   [1. Pumpkin.]
I. Noyed, Robert B.   II. Title.   III. Wonder books (Chanhassen, Minn.)

SB347 .K65   2000
635'.62—dc21   99-055947